The Halloween Secret

written by Dandi
illustrated by Dave Billman

Say! Do you know what happens
On every Halloween?
It's something extra secret
That's seldom ever seen.
The goblins, ghosts, and witches,
Frankensteins and thus,
All dress themselves in costumes
To try to look like us!

Now this is little Ghostie,
And when it's Halloween,
He grabs his shades and blue jeans,
And turns into a *teen*!

On other days our Wanda
Goes flying with her bat.
She wears a cape and black hat,
And plays with her black cat.

But Halloween transforms her,
And in her ballet shoes,
You'd never guess that other days
She whips up witches' brews.

Frankenstein at other times
Is really rather scary.
But check him out on Halloween
When Frank turns into Harry!

Jack O. Lantern looks so tame
On every other night,
Sitting in his pumpkin patch
In the pale moonlight.

But look at Jack on Halloween,
And watch that pumpkin face.
A little leaguer through and through,
Jack covers second base.

Gabe's a goblin through the year.

He likes to haunt and seek.

Screams are music to his ears.

He loves to make us shriek!

But Halloween brings changes,
And if you take a peek,
Beneath his hair and glasses,
Your Gabe becomes a geek.

The witch's cat is last of all
To put on people clothes.
There aren't too many choices left.
Now what do you suppose. . .

So what becomes of this black cat?

A special costume maybe?

There's only one small costume left.

The cat becomes a baby!

And now you know the secret,
That quicker than a wink,
Beneath those people costumes
Are not what people think.
So if you see plain children
On Halloween tonight,
Remember ghosts and witches
Are lurking out of sight.